Time for School, Little Dinosaur

By Gail Herman

Illustrated by
Norman Gorbaty

Random House 🏠 New York

Text copyright © 1990 by Random House, Inc. Illustrations copyright © 1990 by Norman Gorbaty.
All rights reserved. Originally published in different form in 1990 as a
Random House PICTUREBACK® READER. First Random House Jellybean Books™ edition, 1998.
Library of Congress Catalog Card Number: 98-65517 ISBN: 0-679-89211-7 (trade) ; 0-679-98211-1 (lib. bdg.)
www.randomhouse.com/kids/
Printed in the United States of America 10 9 8 7 6 5 4 3 2 1
JELLYBEAN BOOKS is a trademark of Random House, Inc.

Little Dinosaur wakes up.

He packs his book bag.
He packs his lunch box.
He is getting ready for school.

"Little Dinosaur," says Spikey.
"It is summer.
There is no school."

"I am getting ready,"
says Little Dinosaur.
"I am getting ready for school."

Each day
Little Dinosaur
wakes up.

He packs
his book bag.

He packs
his lunch box.

He waits
for the
school bus.

Each day Spikey wakes up.

"It is summer," he says.
"Little Dinosaur is getting ready.
But not me!"

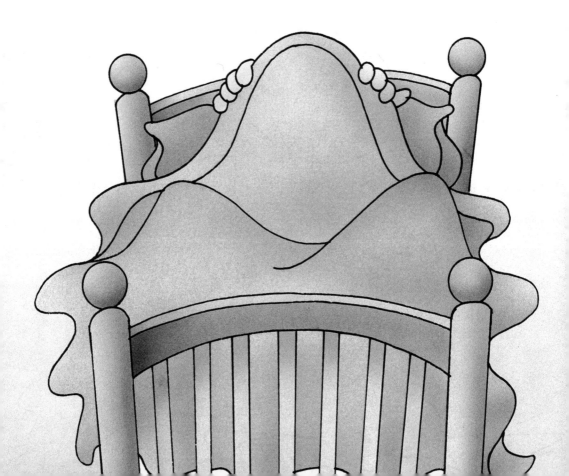

It is time for school.
Little Dinosaur wakes up.
And...he is ready!

Spikey wakes up.
Oh, no!
His book bag is not ready.

Oh, no!
His lunch box is not ready.
Will he be late?

Little Dinosaur waits for the bus.

Here it is.
But where is Spikey?

"Wait!" says Little Dinosaur.
"Wait for Spikey!"

"Here I am!" says Spikey.
"I was not ready.
But tomorrow I will be..."

"Just like Little Dinosaur."